# Pulling Together

## Dawn L. Watkins

Illustrated by Kathy Pflug

JOURNEY
FORTH™

Greenville, South Carolina

Matthew left the table
and ran upstairs.
He came back carrying the sock.
He untied it and
rolled the coins out on the table.

"I've been working some,"
he said.

John Briggs put out his hand
and touched a dime.
He looked at his wife again.
She smiled and tilted her head at him.

Matthew watched,
his heart tripping.

"Well," said his father,
"maybe we could try it."

# 10

## Cherry Springs Fair

The morning was as bright as any
morning Matthew had ever seen.
The field behind the smithy
was full of people.
Sawhorses with boards over them
held pies and quilts
and a thousand other things.
There was a flag flying,
and children raced between
the posts set up for horseshoes.

Addie took her pie and went to the
far side of the field.
Joe Parker went by
and waved at Matthew.
He was walking with the girl
who had liked the puzzle.

Matthew sat atop Ben.
His father and brother were
rubbing the harness with oily cloths
to make it shine.

"Maybe if we win," said Matthew,
"we can buy some new harness."

John Briggs pulled his hand along
a gleaming strap. "And what would we
be needing with new harness?"

"Some with brass on it,"
said Matthew.

John Briggs just shook his head
and smiled his smile.

Matthew slid off Ben.
"Papa, can I go around
and look at the other teams?"

"Don't get lost," said John Briggs.
"Or in the way."

Matthew patted Dolly as he went by.
He passed team after team
of workhorses.
All stood calmly in their places,
as if this were just another day
of logging in the woods.

Then he saw them, the great gray
horses that Joe had talked about.
Bailey's grays.
They shone in the morning sun
like marble statues.

It took his breath away
to see them.

Their chins were far above
the heads of the men
who were brushing them.
Muscles swelled along their
wide shoulders.
And their hooves seemed
as big as church bells.

Matthew's heart both jumped
and sank at the sight of the team.
They were a joy to behold.
But he knew at the same time
that Dolly and Ben had no chance
to win against such animals.

He heard a man laugh.
"Not that I'd be telling you that,"
the man said. "The rule says
'working draft horses,' doesn't it?"

"Since when do you work these
horses, Bailey, I'd like to know?"
The other man's voice
had a laugh in it too.

Then both men laughed together.
Matthew felt his face get hot.
He ran back to his father and Luke.

"Papa," he said,
"I saw Bailey's grays!"

His father and brother had clipped straps to the halters on Dolly and Ben.

"We have to weigh the team in," Luke told him.

"Papa," Matthew said again. "I saw the grays. And I think they're not supposed to be in the contest."

"What, son?" said his father.

"I heard two men talking. I don't think those gray horses work in the woods like ours. Like they have to if they're in the contest."

John Briggs looked across at the grays. The muscles in his jaw pushed in and out. At last he said, "That may be, and it may not be. But it is not for us to go into. Come along, now, to the weighing."

Matthew did as he was told.
He watched as many smaller teams
weighed in on the big platform scale
and were sent to the lightweight class.

Maybe, he thought, maybe
Dolly and Ben will make it into
the lightweight class.
Then they would have a good chance
to win. In fact, he was sure
they could easily win there.

Luke led Dolly and Ben up on
the scale. The man said,
"Well, John, they're heavyweights
by just a hundred pounds."

Matthew's chest felt tight
and his eyes stung.
He felt sorry for his father.
But John Briggs smiled and took
the number plate for his team.

Matthew did not want to watch
the lightweight horses pull
the logs in the first contest.
He wished that they could just go home.

"What's the matter, Matt?" said Luke.

Matthew shook his head.
The first small team came around.
Their harness jingled.

The driver brought the horses
to the front of the logs.
Then he made the horses back up.

The hook on the doubletree
slipped into the ring on the logs.
At once the horses leaped forward.

"Bad," said Luke.
"He should make them wait
'til he says something."

Matthew knew that. He also knew
that the horses should not lunge
into their harness.

Matthew went back to Ben and Dolly.
He petted their noses,
the way his father did.
He loved the team, but today,
just today, he wished his father
owned bigger horses.

A while later, Matthew heard
a long cheer go up from the crowd,
and he knew the lightweight
contest was over.

Soon his father came to get
Ben and Dolly.
His father whistled the tune
he always whistled.

Matthew wondered
at his father's happiness.
Then he thought—
Papa's probably not seen
Bailey's gray horses yet.

John Briggs looked at his son's face.
"Matthew, don't be so worried.
It's only a contest.
If the Lord wants us to win,
we'll win. And if He does not,
it is the same to us.

Every important thing
will still be the same. Yes?"

Matthew nodded, but only because
he knew his father wanted him to.

# 11

## *Round One*

The announcer's voice boomed through the megaphone:
"Log pull for the heavyweight division will begin. These are the teams."

Matthew heard Sam Johnson's name called. Then there was applause.

Another name was called.

There was a quiet moment,
and Matthew knew that
the man was leading his team
into the pull area.
Then there was more applause.
And then another name and more
applause.

The announcer said, "John Briggs."
Matthew's father clicked his tongue
lightly, and he and Ben and Dolly
went out into the ring.

"Weighing in at just
one hundred pounds over the mark
are Ben and Dolly."

The crowd murmured among
themselves. Matthew knew that
they were feeling a little sorry too.

The team looked small beside
the others. The applause was quiet.

"And Grant Bailey," said the announcer.

The crowd gasped as the huge gray team sped into the ring.

Bailey half-ran and half-skidded as he followed behind the horses, holding them in.
Their wide black harness was studded with silver spangles.
They sparkled and jingled.
The horses tossed their heads and snorted as they pranced around the ring.

Matthew looked over at his father and their team. Their harness was plain but well shined, and his father looked tall and calm.

Matthew took a sudden comfort in the tilt of his father's hat.

The contest began.
All five teams easily pulled
the first pile of logs across the line.
No team had even used the whole
two minutes.
Men with two teams
brought two more logs
and chained them to the other logs.

"Now," said the announcer,
"Round two."

Sam Johnson's team barely
made the line in time.
The next team did not make it.
The third team pulled through
just at the bell. John Briggs's team came
to the starting line.

John Briggs brought his horses
to the front of the load
and stopped them.

He leaned over and picked up
the doubletree. He said, "Back now."

Ben and Dolly backed up together.
The hook slipped easily into the ring
on the logs. The time clock began.

John Briggs smoothed the lines
and then clicked his tongue.
The team leaned into the harness.

At first nothing appeared to happen.

After what seemed too long,
the logs began to move.

Ben and Dolly pulled them
half the way to the line
before John Briggs said, "Whoa."
The horses stopped dead still.

John Briggs went around
to the horses' heads.
He stroked their noses
and ran his hand down their front legs.

Finally he went back, picked up
the lines, and clicked to his horses.
The team leaned
into the harness again,
and again the logs slowly,
slowly began to move.
The front ends of the logs passed
the finish line ten seconds
before time ran out.

The crowd cheered wildly.
Matthew and Luke hugged each other
and slapped each other on the back.

Grant Bailey's team
came charging up.
They stamped and pawed the dirt
while the work teams pulled the logs
back to the starting line.

Then the announcer called "Ready."
The man drove his team
to the front of the logs.

"Back up," he yelled at the horses,
but they charged forward.
The man leaped forward
and hauled back on the lines.
"Back up!" he roared, louder than before.

The gray team, their heads bobbing
and their nostrils wide,
backed up jerkily.

Then the ring went over the hook,
and they plunged forward
against the chest harness.

The heavy logs did not move.
The crowd murmured a little,
as if they had felt the sudden tightening
of the harness on their own chests.

"Haw, get up," the man yelled.

He slapped the lines along
the horses' backs.
One horse went forward,
but the other hung back.

"GET UP!" the man thundered.

Matthew winced at the tone.
The other horse went forward
and the logs lurched ahead.

And so the whole pull went,
the man yelling
and slapping down the lines,
the horses jumping and struggling.
They made the time limit.

There was applause,
but it was not loud.

Matthew could see the sweat
and lather on the gray horses
as they went by him.
They were blowing through their noses
in fast snorts. Matthew
looked over at his father.
John Briggs was following
the gray team with his eyes,
and he was not smiling.

The men and teams came
and added a huge log to the pile.

Sam Johnson walked up
and studied the load.
Then he went to the judge
and withdrew his team.

Matthew and Luke
looked at each other. "Will it be
too heavy for Ben and Dolly?"
Matthew asked.

"Papa will know," said Luke.

# 12

## *The Last Pull*

The three remaining teams lined up
according to the times
they had made in the second round.
First was a black team,
then the big gray team,
and then John Briggs's brown team.

The announcer said,
"In this last round,
there is no finish line.

The team that pulls the logs the farthest
in the two minutes will win."

The first team could not
move the logs at all.
After a minute of trying,
the driver unhooked his team.
He tipped his hat toward the audience
and took his team away.

The audience cheered him,
and the announcer said,
"A fine try."

The gray team got hooked up
after a struggle
and lunged to the work.
The driver yelled, "Haw, haw, haw,"
and thrashed the lines.
"Haw," he shouted.
Slap! went the lines.

The horses would not pull together.
One would lunge forward,
then the other.
The heavy logs jerked forward
inch by inch, digging up the ground.
More foam grew on the horses
under their harness,
and they snorted loudly.

"Get up," the man yelled at them.
The gray horses shook
with the strain of pulling.

"PULL!" The man smacked
the lines on their backs.
One horse suddenly sprang backwards.
It stepped out of the traces.
Frightened, it leaped forward.

"They're tangled up!" Luke said.

Matthew thought surely the man
would stop the horses, but he did not.
"Get up!" the driver hollered again.

Matthew could not watch.
He put his forehead against a pole
beside him and looked at his boots.
He could hear the man yelling,
the horses puffing and snorting,
the crowd mumbling.
The fancy harness jingled.

It sounded like coins falling,
Matthew thought.
At last the bell rang.

"It's over," said Luke.

Matthew looked at his brother
and then at the gray team.

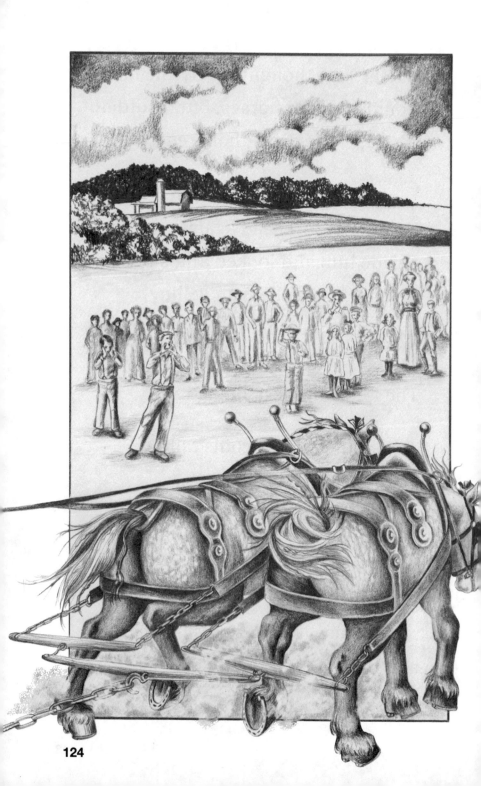

They had pulled the logs almost to
the finish line of the other rounds.
A man put a red marker
where the logs had stopped.
The audience applauded.

Matthew wanted to run out
onto the field.
He wanted to tell his father
not to make Ben and Dolly try it.
But his father had already brought
the team onto the field.
The gray team was leaving.
The whites of their eyes showed
and their sides heaved.

Matthew had never seen horses
look so wild and dangerous.

When the logs were set again,
the announcer said, "Ready."

John Briggs asked his horses
to back up.
He hooked the logs to the team
and straightened the lines.

Matthew held his breath.
Everyone seemed to hold his breath.
There was not so much as a cough
from the crowd.

The man with the watch nodded.
The time began.
John Briggs clicked his tongue.
Ben and Dolly, their ears forward,
pulled together.

Five seconds, then ten seconds went by.
Finally, the logs began to move,
and suddenly they were
moving smoothly.
Ben and Dolly strained against
the heavy load with all their strength.

Matthew lost his ability
to tell time.
It was as if nothing
in the world was moving
but his father, the logs,
and the two small brown horses
with their black manes.

"Whoa," said John Briggs.
Ben and Dolly stopped pulling
and stood still, breathing heavily.
John Briggs went around to their heads
and adjusted their bridles.
He picked up a small stone
and tossed it out of the way.
Then he went back
and picked up the lines.

He clicked his tongue.
The horses leaned mightily
into their harness.

Again after a few seconds,
the logs crept forward.
The two horses pulled together
evenly, steadily.
Their shoulder muscles bulged.
Their nostrils flared.
They pulled until
the veins in their necks stood out.

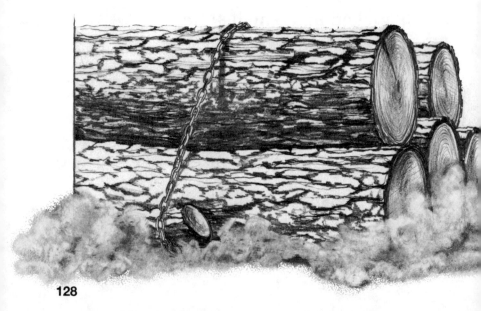

And then it happened.
Dolly's front foot slipped
and she went down on one knee.
She kept pulling even then.
John Briggs said "Ho, ho, there."
The crowd groaned.
Matthew bit his lip.

Dolly stood up and shook her mane.

John Briggs picked up her foot
and looked at it.
He ran his hand down both her legs.
Then he walked ahead of the team,
throwing stones aside
and studying the path
that the gray team had plowed up.

The seconds ticked by.
The only sound
was the puffing of the horses.
John Briggs came back to them,
patted them,
and then returned to the lines.

He clicked his tongue quietly,
and his two horses
leaned into their work.
The logs moved again.

"Matt," said Luke in a whisper,
"I think we might make it."

The man with the watch
called twenty seconds left.
The little team was nearly
to the red marker.
Their sides lathered,
and their breaths came in snorts.
The crowd began a count:
"Twelve, eleven."

Ben and Dolly heaved together
and the logs slid past the red marker.
Matthew's eyes blurred.
His father was still asking the team
to pull. The crowd was on its feet.

"Nine, eight, seven,"
the crowd was chanting.
Matthew clutched his brother's arm.
They both were yelling
but they could not hear themselves.
"Four, three, two."

The crowd was screaming now.
At the last second,
as the bell was ringing,
the front of the logs hit the finish line.

The crowd burst into cheers.
Men threw their hats into the air,
and the applause was louder
than any thunder.

Matthew and Luke
grabbed each other,
pounding each other and laughing.

People were pouring onto the field,
cheering all the way.
For five minutes,
the cheering went on.
Matthew could not see his father
for the crowd around the team.

When at last he could
make himself heard,
the announcer called for the winner
to come get his trophy
and the prize money.

There was a pause.
The crowd pulled back
so that John Briggs could
get his horses through.

But instead of driving them
toward the judge's stand,
he took them toward the other end.
Everyone watched in silence.

John Briggs brought the team
around in front of his sons.
He handed the lines to Matthew.
"Let's all go get that trophy."

Matthew took the lines.
John Briggs and Luke walked together
behind him. And together,
like heroes home from war,
they all walked the field, just as they did
every day when their work was done.
And at that moment, John Briggs's horses
did not look small at all.